Enchanted Collection

Stories and Activities to Empower Young Princesses

we make books come alive®
pi kids **Phoenix International Publications, Inc.**
Chicago • London • New York • Hamburg • Mexico City • Paris • Sydney

Edited by Erin Rose Wage and Veronica Wagner
Illustrated by Art Mawhinney, Megan Roldan, Jaime Diaz Studios,
and the Disney Storybook Art Team
Book design by Kathleen Cosgriff

Published by Phoenix International Publications, Inc.
8501 West Higgins Road   59 Gloucester Place
Chicago, Illinois 60631   London W1U 8JJ

www.pikidsmedia.com

p i kids and *we make books come alive* are trademarks of Phoenix International Publications, Inc.,
and are registered in the United States.

Look and Find is a trademark of Phoenix International Publications, Inc., and
is registered in the United States and Canada.

8 7 6 5 4 3 2 1

ISBN: 978-1-5037-5075-3

Table of Contents

Cinderella

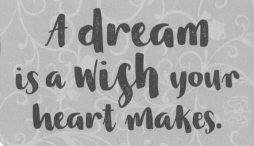

A dream is a wish your heart makes.

Cinderella never gets a moment's peace! She's up at dawn, every day, cooking and cleaning for her selfish stepmother and stepsisters. Cinderella dreams of happier days...but will they ever come?

Princess Words
An **invitation** is a written or spoken offer to go somewhere or do something.

One day, an **invitation** arrives from the palace. It's for a royal ball. Cinderella can't wait to go! But, on the big day, her jealous stepsisters destroy her party dress. With nothing to wear, Cinderella will have to stay home.

Or will she? Luckily, Cinderella has a fairy godmother! Dressed in a magical gown and glass slippers, Cinderella rides to the palace.

Princess Words
When dancers **waltz**, they step in a *one*-two-three rhythm as they turn around and around on the dance floor.

The spell will last only until midnight. Long before the clock strikes, during **waltz** after waltz, Cinderella and the Prince fall in love.

However, when the clock does strike, Cinderella must rush away. In her hurry, she accidentally leaves behind one glass slipper—and does not leave her name! Back at home, she is

dressed in rags again, with a single souvenir: the second glass slipper.

When the Prince tries to find the girl whose foot fits the lost slipper, Cinderella's cruel stepmother locks her in her room and breaks the slipper carried by the royal messenger.

Cinderella escapes—and the second slipper fits perfectly! She has found her true love.

Picture Puzzle

Bibbidi-bobbidi-boo! Cinderella's Fairy Godmother will get her to the palace—in a fashionable coach that looks nothing like a pumpkin!

Find 10 differences in this charming scene.

Answer key: horse, dog, sparkles, curtains, "C" monogram, top of carriage, Cinderella, mouse, mouse's hat, three sparkles

Look and Find

Cinderella waltzes across the dance floor, enjoying the music and the company at her royal ball. She wants all the guests to enjoy themselves, so she has made special accommodations for the tiniest of her friends. It just wouldn't be a ball without them! While the dancers count their steps, look for Cinderella's animal companions:

Jaq

Luke

Mary

Suzy

Gus

Bert

Ariel

You're not getting cold fins, are you?

Under the sea, a mermaid named Ariel longs to be part of the human world above. One day, a storm wrecks a ship she is watching. Ariel saves a passenger, Prince Eric, and sings to him until help arrives.

When Ariel's father, King Triton, discovers what his daughter has done, he **forbids** her to go to the surface again. Humans are dangerous!

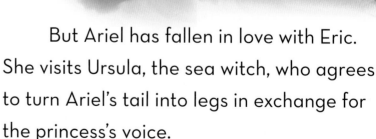

Princess Words

If someone **forbids** you to do something, they are ordering you not to do it.

But Ariel has fallen in love with Eric. She visits Ursula, the sea witch, who agrees to turn Ariel's tail into legs in exchange for the princess's voice.

Ariel agrees. The spell gives her three days to get a kiss from Eric in order to remain human. If she fails, she will return to the sea and belong to Ursula forever.

When human Ariel appears on the beach, Eric doesn't remember her. But in spite of her silence, he soon grows fond of this unusual girl.

Furious, Ursula changes herself into a woman named Vanessa. Using Ariel's voice, she puts a spell on Eric, and the prince asks Vanessa to marry him.

Ariel's animal friends spring into action, breaking the **nautilus** shell necklace that holds the princess's voice and the spell over Eric. Now Ariel can speak, and Eric recognizes his true love. He defeats Ursula and saves his mermaid princess...and King Triton makes Ariel human so she can live happily ever after, on land!

Princess Words
A **nautilus** is an aquatic creature with a spiral-chambered shell.

Look and Find

Ariel collects things from the human world as she dreams about life on dry land. Can you find these treasures from her collection?

"dinglehopper"

pipe

birdcage

violin

compass

boot

Picture Puzzle

Ariel likes human objects...
but she doesn't always
know how to use them.

Comb through these scenes to find 10 differences.

Answer key: Eric's beverage, spoon, "E" monogram, fruit, candle, Sebastian, Ariel's glass, birds, sun, fork

Mulan

I have to do something.

The Huns are invading Fa Mulan's homeland, China! The Emperor commands one man from each household to join the army to defeat them. Mulan doesn't want her ailing father to go, so she disguises herself as a man and heads to the army camp in his place. The Fa family's **ancestors** know Mulan needs protection. So Mushu, a tiny **dragon**, goes with her.

Princess Words

An **ancestor** is a person related to you who lived a long time ago, like your great-great-great grandmother.

Princess Words

A **dragon** is a legendary creature. In China, dragons are a symbol of power, strength, and good luck.

After a rocky start at the camp, Mulan becomes a skilled warrior. In a mountain battle with the Huns, she saves Commander Li Shang's life by starting an avalanche that buries the enemies' troops. Li Shang is grateful, and pardons Mulan when he discovers she isn't a man, after all.

Still, one loss won't stop the Huns. General Shan Yu and the remains of his army invade the Imperial City and capture the Emperor. Mulan helps her soldier friends slip into the palace, and the final battle for China begins. In a thrilling rooftop duel, Mulan and Mushu defeat Shan Yu, the Emperor is freed, and China is saved!

Mulan's family is happy to have her home again. When Li Shang appears at the gate, Mulan, proud of who she is and what she has done, asks him to dinner. Li Shang is happy to accept the invitation.

Picture Puzzle

Whoops! Mulan may need a little more practice.

Swing around and find 10
differences in these training scenes.

Answer key: Mulan's stick, Cri-kee, warrior's legs, bug, arrow with fruit, water in bucket, Chien-Po's belt,
arrow on ground, warrior's hair band, rock.

Look and Find

Mulan is a hero! She helped save her country. Can you find the friends who wish her a safe journey home to her family?

Cri-Kee

Chien-Po

Ling

Mushu

the Emperor

Little Brother

Snow White

*I really feel quite **happy** now. Everything's going to be all right.*

In a faraway castle, there lives a princess named Snow White. The cruel Queen, her stepmother, looks into a magic mirror and learns that Snow White is the most beautiful one in all the land. The jealous Queen orders her servant to take Snow White into the forest, never to return!

Princess Words
A **cottage** is a small, simple house.

Lost in the forest, Snow White makes new friends. The kind woodland creatures guide her to a cozy little **cottage**, home to Seven Dwarfs.

The equally kind Dwarfs ask Snow White to stay with them. She is happy there with her Dwarf and animal friends!

The next day, the mirror tells the Queen that Snow White is still the fairest. This time, the Queen decides to do away with her stepdaughter for good!

The Queen disguises herself as an old woman. She tricks Snow White into eating an apple that has been poisoned with a magic spell. Snow White falls into a deep, deep **slumber**. Only True Love's Kiss will wake her.

The Dwarfs want to help their friend. They must find Snow White's true love. And they do! A handsome Prince whom Snow White met earlier soon arrives... and wakes Snow White. Now Snow White, the Prince, and the Seven Dwarfs can live happily ever after.

Princess Words
A **slumber** is a state of deep sleep.

Look and Find

Snow White found a place to hide from the evil Queen, but it belongs to seven very untidy Dwarfs. It's time to clean up! Help Snow White straighten up by finding these out-of-place belongings:

Bashful's toy hedgehog

Happy's treasure chest

Grumpy's rocks

Doc's inkwell

Sleepy's blanket

Sneezy's flowers

Dopey's alarm clock

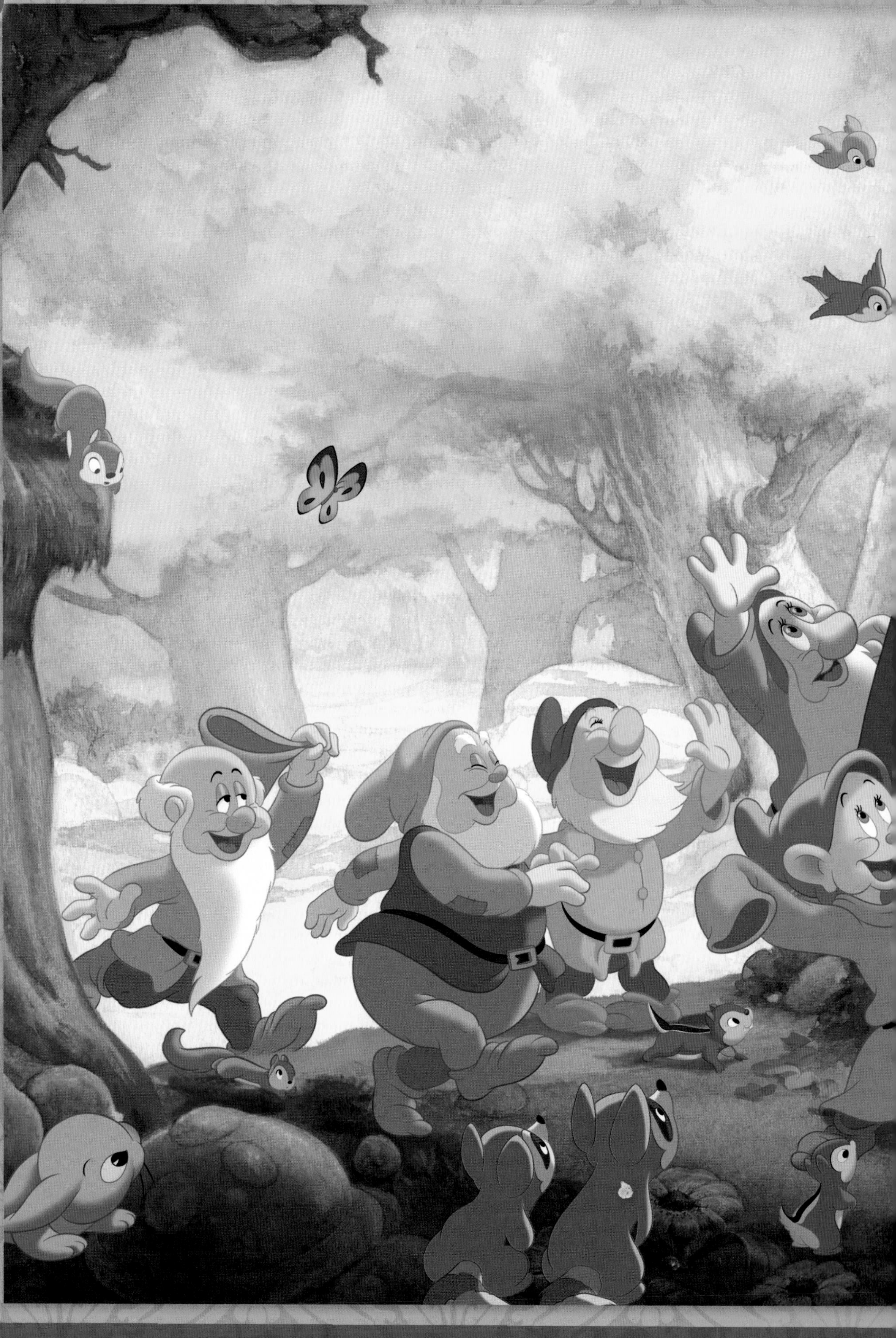

Look and Find

Deep in the friendly forest,
   you'll find many orange things:
Trees with orange leaves,
   and a little butterfly's wings!

Find these *orange* things:

squirrel

bird

butterfly

bunny

leaves

Look and Find

What a lovely day for a picnic! There's something here for everyone, even the royal horses. Do you see these treats a horse would enjoy?

bag of bran

sugar cubes

horse biscuit

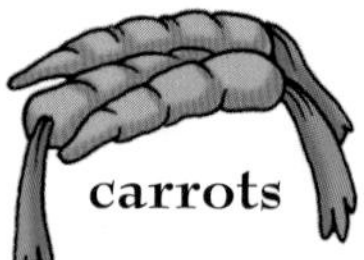

carrots

bowl of oats

corn

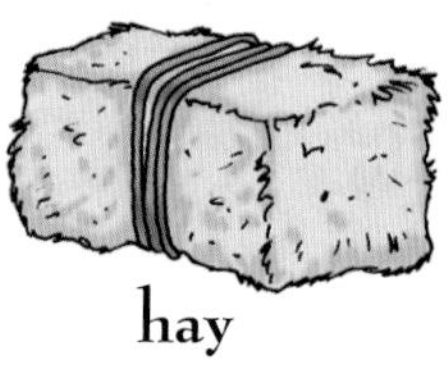

hay

Tiana

The only way to get what you want in this world is through **hard work.**

Ever since she was little, Tiana has dreamed of opening a restaurant. She has worked hard to try to make her dream come true.

Tiana's friend Charlotte has always dreamed of marrying a prince. So she invites Prince Naveen to her **Mardi Gras** ball.

Naveen doesn't dream of restaurants or princesses. He dreams of finding his fortune.

Princess Words
Mardi Gras occurs the Tuesday before the start of Lent. It is a festive celebration during which people dress up, have parades, and make merry.

Before the ball, evil Dr. Facilier changes the prince into a frog! The only way Naveen will change back is with a princess's kiss.

When Naveen sees Tiana at the ball, dressed in a beautiful gown and tiara, he thinks she is a princess! Naveen promises to buy Tiana a restaurant in exchange for a kiss.

But Naveen doesn't turn back into a prince. Instead, Tiana **transforms** into a frog!

The two frogs have one more chance. Charlotte is the princess of Mardi Gras until the parade ends at midnight. If she kisses Naveen before then, the frogs will turn back into humans.

Tiana and Naveen race to the parade, but they're too late. Mardi Gras is over.

Princess Words
To **transform** means to change the structure of something.

Even though they are frogs, Tiana and Naveen fall in love. They decide to get married.

Because Naveen is a prince, once he and Tiana marry, Tiana becomes a princess. She kisses Naveen—and they both turn back into humans! Tiana and Naveen open a restaurant and fulfill their dreams together, living *hoppily* ever after.

Look and Find

Tiana and her friends have arrived at the home of Mama Odie, the blind 197-year-old good magic lady. While Mama Odie determines what the frogs need, look around the galley of her old shrimp boat for these things she needs:

jar of candy

Juju

this jar of powder

hot sauce

this magic potion

gourd

Picture Puzzle

Tiana and Naveen are on a mission!

Do you see 10 differences between these bayou scenes?

Answer key: white flower, missing firefly, tree, Ray, big lily pad, palm frond, Louis's tooth, flopped firefly, lily pad in background, algae

Look and Find

All of Tiana's dreams seem to be coming true! First she found her prince, and now she has opened her restaurant. Look around the busy dining room for these items every great restaurant should have:

opening day photo

menu

banner

reservation book

newspaper review

lucky horsehoe

Grand
pening

Rapunzel

*I have **magic** hair that glows when I sing.*

Golden-haired Rapunzel lives in a tall tower hidden from the world. She is always dreaming about the world outside. But Mother Gothel says it is too dangerous for Rapunzel to explore.

One day, Flynn Rider, a thief, is looking for a place to hide. When he climbs into the tower, Rapunzel ties him up—and makes him a deal.

Princess Words
A **satchel** is another word for a small bag, often with a shoulder strap.

If Flynn will show her the world outside, Rapunzel will return the crown she has found in his **satchel**. Flynn is reluctant, but he agrees.

As they travel, Flynn learns a secret about Rapunzel: her hair has magical powers.

Years ago, Mother Gothel took Rapunzel from her parents, the King and Queen. Rapunzel's magical hair keeps Mother Gothel young. That's why she has kept Rapunzel locked in the tower.

Now, Mother Gothel tricks Rapunzel into returning to the tower. When Flynn arrives to rescue her, Gothel wounds him.

Rapunzel tries to heal Flynn, but he cuts off her long **locks** to free her from Mother Gothel forever. It works, but Flynn is hurt badly.

Rapunzel heals Flynn with one magical golden tear.

Soon *Princess* Rapunzel is reunited with her royal parents!

Princess Words
Locks are the hairs that grow from your head.

Look and Find

When she was a baby, Rapunzel was stolen and locked in a tower by a mean and vain woman named Mother Gothel, who uses Rapunzel's magical hair to stay young. Since Rapunzel is never allowed outside the tower, she finds other ways to keep busy. Do you see some of her favorite things?

pottery

knitting needles

darts

book

puzzle

puppet

guitar

ballet shoes

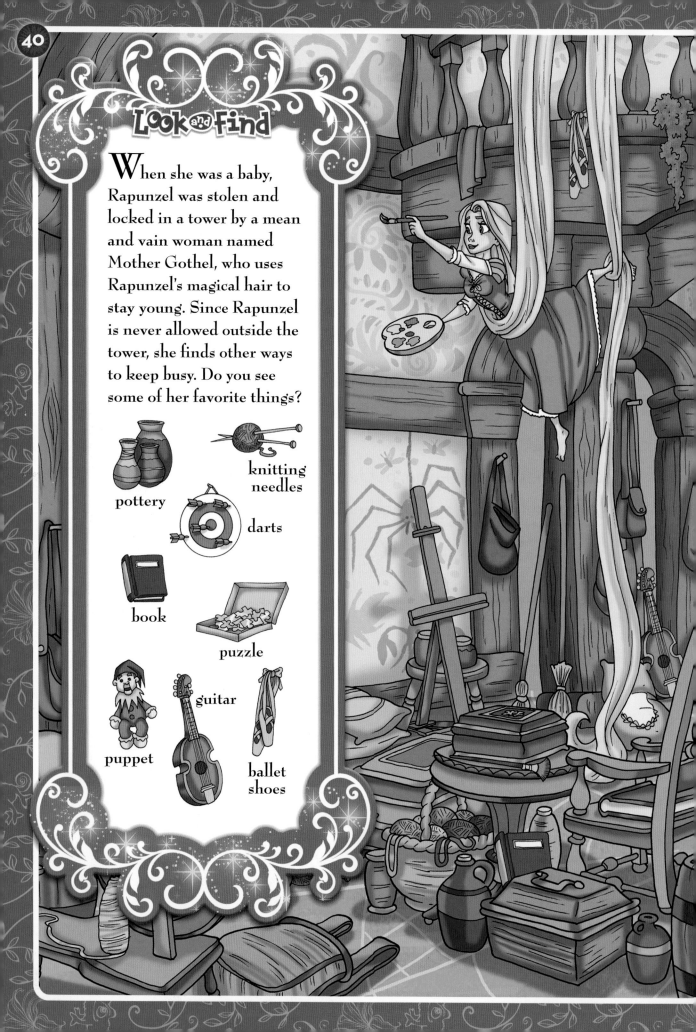

Picture Puzzle

Ready…set…go! Rapunzel and Flynn are off to the kingdom.

Search for 10 differences between these speedy scenes.

Look and Find

Rapunzel has persuaded Flynn Rider to take her to see the mysterious lanterns that always appear on her birthday. On the way, they've stopped at the Snuggly Duckling. There, they meet some ruffians with surprising dreams. Can you find these thugs in the pub?

Ulf

Hook Hand

Attila

Killer

bartender

Tor

Bruiser

Pocahontas

This is the path I choose. What will yours be?

When John Smith and his shipmates arrive in North America, they claim the land for the King of England. They want to dig for gold, which is the most valuable thing that the land has to offer—valuable to *them*, that is.

Princess Words
The **Powhatan** are a nation of Native American people from Virginia.

Pocahontas, a young **Powhatan** woman, is curious about these visitors. She feels her future may be connected to John Smith. So she paddles her **canoe** deep into the woods to talk with Grandmother Willow, a tree spirit.

Grandmother Willow tells Pocahontas that if she listens with her heart, she will know what to do.

Princess Words
A **canoe** is a light and narrow boat, pointed at both ends, that is usually moved by paddle.

Pocahontas teaches John Smith about the earth's *other* valuable things. She shows him how creatures are our friends, and the trees, rocks, and rivers have a spirit as well as a name.

John Smith begins to understand. But his shipmates do not.

The English treat the land badly, cutting down the forest and ignoring its creatures. This upsets the Powhatan. They want the English to leave.

When Pocahontas listens to her heart, she knows that she and John Smith can help their people live together peacefully.

Look and Find

Pocahontas is listening. She is tracking an animal that got into her village's supply of corn. The trail is not the only thing she is following. By helping her people, Pocahontas is also following her heart. Help Pocahontas pick up the trail that the corn thief left behind:

Meeko

this partially eaten corncob

fur

broken branch

scratched bark

paw prints

Picture Puzzle

First meetings can be magical!

Look for 10 differences around Pocahontas and John.

Answer key: Flit, canoe, scarlet leaf, Pocahontas's belt, Pocahontas's hair, John Smith's boots, yellow leaf, grass, tree branch, John Smith's armor

Aurora

They say if you dream a thing more than once, it's sure to come true!

Deep within the forest, Briar Rose lives in a hidden cottage with her three aunts—Flora, Fauna, and Merryweather.

What Briar Rose doesn't know is that she's actually a *princess* named **Aurora**! Her "aunts" are good fairies who protect her from an evil spell that the wicked Maleficent cast upon her when she was born.

One day, as Prince Phillip rides through the forest, he hears Aurora's beautiful singing. Phillip stops to talk with Aurora, and the two laugh, dance, and fall in love. They agree to meet again later that evening.

Princess Words

An **aurora** is a group of bands of light that appear in the sky. **Aurora** is also the Latin word for "dawn."

But when Aurora returns home, the fairies tell her the truth. Tonight they will take her back to the castle to meet her parents and to celebrate her birthday.

There, Maleficent once again uses her evil magic on Aurora.

Under Maleficent's spell, the princess pricks her finger on a **spinning wheel** and falls into a deep sleep!

Princess Words
A **spinning wheel** is a mechanical device used to twist together raw fibers to make string or yarn.

With help from Flora, Fauna, and Merryweather, Prince Phillip charges through a forest of thorns to battle Maleficent—defeating her once and for all.

Princess Aurora awakens, and she and Prince Phillip live happily ever after.

Look and Find

Today is Briar Rose's sixteenth birthday. Her forest friends have thrown her a party. Just look and see all these wonderful gifts they have made:

acorn earrings

wall plaque

walking stick

upside-down cake

bracelet

birthday crown

berry necklace

Picture Puzzle

Aurora and Phillip dance the day away!

Catch all 10 differences in these two scenes.

Jasmine

I am not a prize to be won!

In the faraway land of Agrabah, Princess Jasmine dreams of life outside the palace walls.

Her father, the **Sultan**, reminds Jasmine that she must marry a prince before her next birthday, in three days! So she sneaks out of the palace to the market. There, a fruit seller accuses her of stealing—and a peasant named Aladdin whisks Jasmine to the safety of his hideout.

Princess Words
A **sultan** is a ruler of a nation, like a king.

Jasmine thanks the boy and begins to trust him. Their lives seem quite similar!

Suddenly, palace guards burst in and arrest Aladdin! They call him a thief. Jasmine commands them to stop, but the guards have orders from Jafar, the Sultan's wicked adviser.

Meanwhile, many princes visit the palace, hoping to marry Jasmine. One, named Prince Ali, arrives on a magic carpet. At first, Jasmine thinks he's just like all the other arrogant princes. But when he takes Jasmine on a magic carpet ride, Ali begins to seem very familiar.

Jasmine happily decides to marry Prince Ali. But Jafar has hypnotized the Sultan. Now Jasmine must marry Jafar!

With help from a **genie**, Ali—who's really Aladdin!—returns to defeat Jafar. The grateful Sultan tells Jasmine she may marry whomever she wants.

"I choose you, Aladdin," says the princess.

Princess Words

A **genie** is a magical spirit who grants wishes.

Picture Puzzle

Will Aladdin's new ride impress Princess Jasmine? It might…or might not!

Join the parade and find 10 differences between these pictures.

Look and Find

Jasmine and Aladdin race to help a friend on the other side of Agrabah. When they're done, they'll have to come back to help clean up the marketplace! Give them a head start by spotting this muddled merchandise:

this basket of apples

this pot

this cloth

this vase

this rug

these dates

Merida

I am Merida, first-born descendant of clan DunBroch, and I'll be shooting for my own hand!

Princess Words

A **clan** is a group of families who all share a common ancestor.

Merida is the spirited, adventurous princess of the **clan** DunBroch. Her father, King Fergus, is adventurous too. But her mother, Queen Elinor, is always trying to teach Merida how to be a proper princess.

Merida isn't interested in playing the **lyre**, weaving a tapestry, or marrying the son of a lord.

"I'm not going to be like you!" Merida tells the queen. There *must* be a way to make her mum understand her.

At the cottage of an old witch, Merida thinks she has found that way. But the Witch's magic doesn't work in the way Merida expects. It changes Queen Elinor into a bear!

Princess Words

A **lyre** is a string instrument, similar to the harp, with a U-shaped frame.

Now Merida must find a way to undo the spell—and keep her bear-hunting father away from his enchanted wife. Once she is discovered, the hunt is on!

Fergus and his friends surround Elinor-Bear. But before Merida can act, the ferocious bear Mor'du appears! Elinor-Bear charges, protecting Merida. The two bears fight a mighty battle, and Mor'du is defeated.

"I just want you back!" Merida cries to her mum. "I love you!" As they hug, the spell dissolves. Elinor returns to her human self, and the bond of love and understanding between mother and daughter is mended.

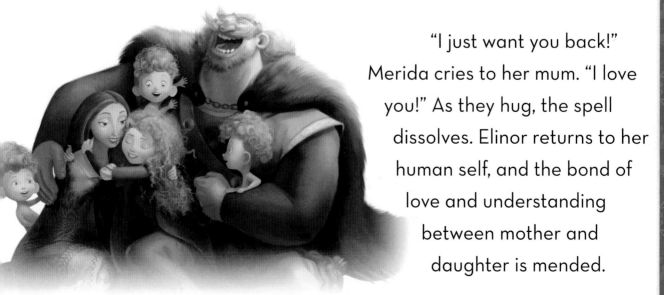

Look and Find

When three neighboring clans come to visit, they play traditional Highland games. Search for the three lords who are the heads of the clans. Then find their three sons, who will compete for Merida's hand in marriage:

Young MacGuffin

Wee Dingwall

Lord Dingwall

Young Macintosh

Lord Macintosh

Lord MacGuffin

Look and Find

Will o' the wisps lead Merida to a witch's cottage, where she asks for a spell to make her mother change. Search the cottage for these things the Witch will need:

mortar & pestle

this secret ingredient

welding mask

tongs

measuring spoon

dried herbs

Picture Puzzle

Merida is brave, and her mother is proud of her!

Look for 10 differences between
these tapestry scenes.

Belle

It's my first time in an enchanted castle!

Belle loves to read. Gaston, a hunter from her small town, wonders why she doesn't love him instead. Belle thinks he is boring and selfish.

When Belle's father, Maurice, gets lost in the woods, he finds a castle covered in **gargoyles** that belongs to a scary Beast. The Beast imprisons Maurice! Belle bravely sets out to save him.

The Beast frightens Belle. But she loves her father so much she takes his place and promises to stay with the Beast in his **enchanted** castle forever.

The spell on the castle and all who live there will break only when the Beast learns to love and finds someone to love him in return.

Princess Words
A **gargoyle** is a strange-looking animal or human sculpture that is found on the roof of a building and that often serves as a water spout.

Princess Words
When something is **enchanted**, it is under a magic spell.

Slowly, Belle and the Beast begin to spend more time together. Belle sees a side of the Beast that she hasn't seen

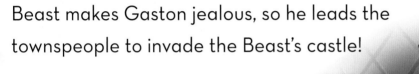

before. The Beast cares for Belle so much that when his magic mirror reveals her father in trouble, the Beast tells Belle to go to him.

Belle returns to town and rescues her father. Hearing Belle describe her friendship with the Beast makes Gaston jealous, so he leads the townspeople to invade the Beast's castle!

When Belle rushes back to the castle and sees the Beast has been wounded, she realizes that she has fallen in love with him. Belle's love breaks the spell! The Beast transforms back into a Prince, and the two live happily ever after.

Look and Find

Belle's father Maurice has a head full of ideas for new inventions, and a workshop full of strange gadgets, gizmos, and contraptions. Some of them even work! Belle thinks her father is a genius. Comb through the clutter and find these irregular inventions:

Personal Page Peruser

Automated Pillow Plumper with "Choose Your Snooze" Action (patent pending)

Double-Triple Doodad, with (optional) Whizzing Whirligig

Three-Scoop Strolling Seed Sower

Press-and-Play Harmonica Helper

Blast-o-Matic Berry Dryer

Look and Find

Though the Beast seems chilly and unkind, his servants are determined to make Belle feel at home. Her first dinner in the castle is an extravaganza of skipping spoons, spinning plates, and fantastic food. "Be our guest!" say Lumiere and his friends. Can you find these tasty tidbits?

reel-y fresh fish

sizeable sundae

prettified pineapple

feathered fowl

combustible confection

cavorting crustacean

Picture Puzzle

True love has broken a beastly spell!

Find 10 differences between these two pictures.

Sometimes Belle is sad to reach the end of a good book. So she leaves herself a little note... and *smiles*.

Smile and turn to the first page for another adventure!

The end